# Keep Trying
# Little Zebra!

Written by Christina Wilsdon
Illustrations by Eugene Komzolov

Reader's Digest Young Families, Inc.

Little Zebra ran as fast as he could across the grassland.

"Wait up!" he shouted to the zebras speeding ahead of him. But they left him behind in a cloud of dust. Little Zebra flopped to the ground. "I give up!" he cried.

"What's wrong, Little Zebra?" asked his mother.

"I can't run as fast as the others!" he said. "I'm tired of being the youngest in the herd."

"You will grow older," said his mother, "and you will get faster."

"But I can't wait that long," said Little Zebra. "I want to be faster *now*!"

"Just keep trying," said his mother. "Maybe you can find other animals to practice with for a little while."

"That's a good idea," said Little Zebra. "I'll go right now and find someone to run with."

Little Zebra met a tortoise under a tree.
"Will you race with me?" asked Little Zebra.
"Sorry," chuckled the tortoise. "I can't run.
My shell is too heavy. Try asking a baby ostrich!"

Little Zebra found a baby ostrich.

"Will you race with me?" asked Little Zebra.

"You bet!" said the ostrich.

"Whew!" puffed Little Zebra. "She's tiny, but she's fast!"

The ostrich ran through the grass, always two steps ahead of Little Zebra.

"Maybe I should just give up," thought Little Zebra. But then he remembered his mother's words, "Keep trying." The next day Little Zebra raced the baby ostrich again—and this time, he won! He pranced with joy, then trotted off to find someone else to race.

Soon Little Zebra spotted a young giraffe.
"Will you race with me?" he asked.
"Sure!" said the giraffe. "Let's run to that tree."
"His legs are taller than I am!" puffed Little
Zebra as he galloped after the giraffe. "This is
hard work. Maybe I should just give up."

But Little Zebra didn't give up. Instead, he tried harder.

Every day for a week, the two animals raced. Each day, Little Zebra galloped a little faster. Finally they ran side by side.

"I may win by a neck for now," laughed the giraffe, "but keep trying, and someday you will win by a nose!"

Little Zebra met a gnu at the water hole.
"Will you race with me?" asked Little Zebra.
"Okay!" said the gnu.

The speedy gnu zipped around the water hole with Little Zebra a few steps behind.

"It's no use," thought Little Zebra. "I'm just a slowpoke!"

Then Little Zebra remembered his races with the giraffe. "I did a good job of catching up with him," he thought. "If I give up now, I'll never get faster."

A few days later, Little Zebra inched past the gnu.

"You're ready to race a gazelle!" the gnu said.

Little Zebra approached a young gazelle.
"Will you race with me?" he asked.

"Ready, set, go!" replied the gazelle. Off
they zoomed.

Little Zebra could not pass her. Tears came
to his eyes as he struggled to keep up.

"Keep trying, Little Zebra," called the gazelle.
"You are the fastest little zebra I've ever seen!"

"Really?" asked Little Zebra in surprise.
"But you're faster. I can't get ahead of you!"

"Only a cheetah can outrun me!" said the
gazelle.

Little Zebra spied a cheetah asleep on a rock. Her cub played nearby. "Could I keep up with a cheetah?" he wondered.

"Will you race with me?" he asked the cub.

The cub padded over to Little Zebra. He blinked up at him, then rolled over on his back, laughing.

"I'm so small and you're so big," said the cub. "I won't be able to run fast until I'm older!"

"Don't worry. You will grow—and you will get faster," said Little Zebra. "And practice helps. Just keep trying!"

Saying this made Little Zebra feel very grown-up!

Little Zebra trotted back to his herd. "I've tried my best, and I've grown some, too," he thought. "Today I'll see if I can race with zebras!"

When the other zebras began running, Little Zebra ran too. They zoomed and zipped, zigged and zagged.

This time, Little Zebra was able to keep up and was surrounded by all his zebra friends.

A baby zebra can have black or brown stripes and can run on its own when it is just an hour old!

Not all zebras look white with black or brown stripes. Some rare zebras are black with patchy white stripes!

No two zebras have exactly the same pattern of stripes. This is similar to the way every person has different fingerprints.